THERE'S NO SUCH THING

AS A

DRAGON

THERE'S NO SUCH THING

AS A

DRAGON

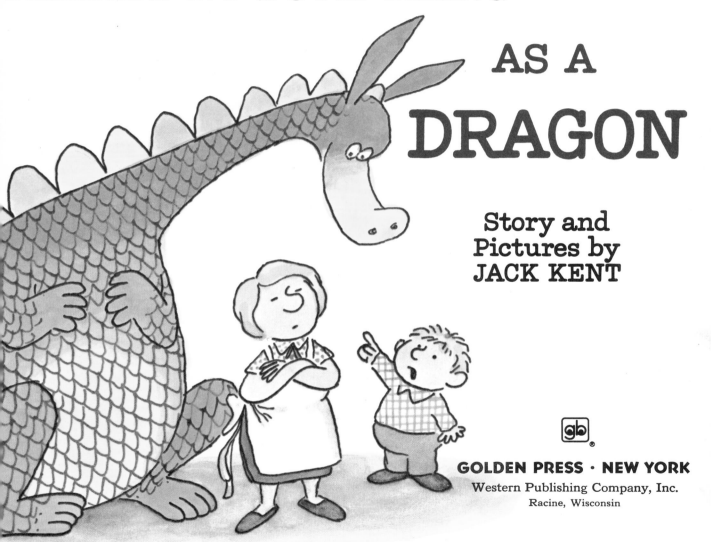

Story and Pictures by JACK KENT

GOLDEN PRESS · NEW YORK
Western Publishing Company, Inc.
Racine, Wisconsin

c. 73

Billy Bixbee was rather surprised when he woke up one morning and found a dragon in his room.

It was a small dragon, about the size of a kitten.

The dragon wagged its tail happily when Billy patted its head.

Billy went downstairs to tell his mother.

"There's no such thing as a dragon!" said Billy's mother. And she said it like she meant it.

Billy went back to his room and began to dress. The dragon came close to Billy and wagged its tail. But Billy didn't pat it. If there's no such thing as something, it's silly to pat it on the head.

Billy washed his face and hands and went
down to breakfast. The dragon went along.
It was bigger now, almost the size of a dog.

Billy sat down at the table.

The dragon sat down ON the table.

This sort of thing was not usually permitted, but there wasn't much Billy's mother could do about it. She had already said there was no such thing as a dragon. And if there's no such thing, you can't tell it to get down off the table.

Mother made some pancakes for Billy, but the dragon ate them all.

Mother made some more.
But the dragon ate those, too.

Mother kept making pancakes until she ran out of batter.

Billy only got one of them, but he said that's all he really wanted, anyway.

Billy went upstairs to brush his teeth. Mother started clearing the table. The dragon, who was quite as big as Mother by this time, made himself comfortable on the hall rug and went to sleep.

By the time Billy came back downstairs the dragon had
grown so much he filled the hall. Billy had to go around by
way of the living room, to get to where his mother was.

"I didn't know dragons grew so fast!" said Billy.

"There's no such thing as a dragon!" said Mother firmly.

Cleaning the downstairs took Mother all morning,
what with the dragon in the way . . .

and having to climb in and out of windows to get from room to room.

By noon the dragon filled the house. Its head hung out the front door, its tail hung out the back door, and there wasn't a room in the house that didn't have some part of the dragon in it.

When the dragon awoke from his nap he was hungry.

A bakery truck went by. The smell of fresh bread was more than the dragon could resist.

The dragon ran down the street after the bakery truck.

The house went along, of course, like the shell on a snail.

BUTTERCUP
BREAD

BREAD

910

The mailman was just coming up the path with some mail for the Bixbees when their house rushed past him and headed down the street.

He chased the Bixbees' house for a few blocks, but he couldn't catch it.

When Mr. Bixbee came home for lunch, the first thing he noticed was that the house was gone.

Luckily, one of the neighbors was able to tell him which way it went.

Mr. Bixbee got in his car and went looking for the house. He studied all the houses as he drove along.

Finally he saw one that looked familiar. Billy and Mrs. Bixbee were waving from an upstairs window.

Mr. Bixbee climbed
over the dragon's head,
onto the porch roof, and
through the upstairs
window.

"How did this happen?" Mr. Bixbee asked.

"It was the dragon," said Billy.

"There's no such thing . . ." Mother started to say.

"There IS a dragon!" Billy insisted. "A very BIG dragon!"
And Billy patted the dragon on the head.

The dragon wagged its tail happily. Then, even faster than it had grown, the dragon started getting smaller.

Soon it was kitten-size again.

"I don't mind dragons THIS size," said Mother. "Why did it have to grow so BIG?"

"I'm not sure," said Billy, "but I think it just wanted to be noticed."

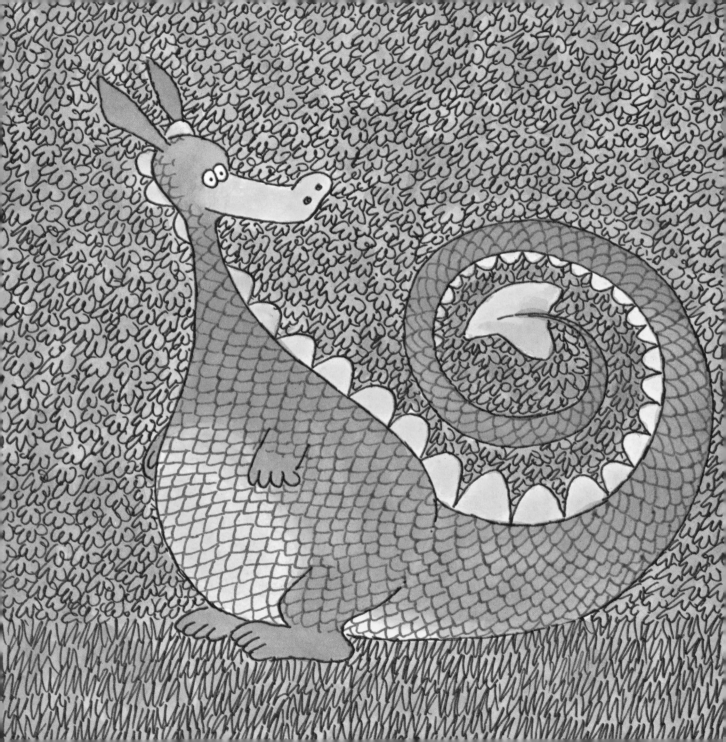